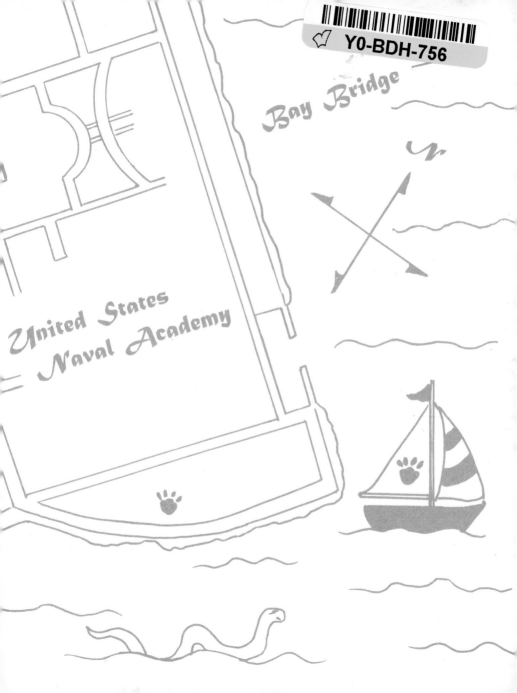

Y0-BDH-756

Bay Bridge

United States
Naval Academy

Doodle
Discovers
Annapolis

Doodle Discovers Annapolis
by Julie Roskin

Illustrations by Alice Yeager

Designed by   Spirit Creative Services

Published by   Eastwind Publishing
               Annapolis, MD

Copyright © 1999 by Julie Roskin
ISBN: 1-885457-14-6

Printed in China

Summary
A small dog experiences the "joy of discovery" when
he visits Annapolis with his family. Follow Doodle
as he explores the friendliness, beauty, history and
charm that make Annapolis such a uniquely
wonderful place.

Category Information
1. Dogs - fiction   2. Discovery   3. History
4. Family   5. Sailing   6. Adventure
7. Animals - fiction

Doodle
Discovers

ANNAPOLIS

by Julie Roskin   Illustrations by Alice Yeager

On this Saturday, Doodle woke up extra early.

And he was very excited!

He ran from room to room to wake up the rest of the family.

Everyone washed and dressed and ate breakfast quickly,

because today was a special day.

They were going to explore Annapolis

the historic seaport and capital of Maryland.

The sun was shining brightly and a gentle breeze was blowing
as they drove over the Chesapeake Bay Bridge.

It was the biggest bridge Doodle had ever seen!
elow, Doodle could see many, many boats and sails of all colors.

Annapolis was crowded but they found a parking space just outside one of the Naval Academy gates.

Doodle was excited to see some of the midshipman marching across the field.

UNITED STATES
NAVAL ACADEMY
FOUNDED 1845

From there,
they walked over to St. John's College

and watched the students
play a game of croquet on the lawn
next to the 400 year old Liberty Tree.

Doodle had never seen this game before and was very
interested.

Doodle led the way as they walked over to State Circle to see the State House with its beautiful shining dome.

The state flag of Maryland on top of the dome waved in the breeze.

Next they toured Main Street.

the shops were open and Doodle stopped to look in the windows. One of the shop owners even came out to give him a treat!

All of a sudden Doodle could see the tops of sailboats and headed for the city dock.

Doodle and his family were delighted to find
a captain of one of the sailboats offering rides to visitors

When it was his turn to go aboard,
Doodle trotted up the stairs to the boat
and waited to have his lifejacket put on.

With everyone seated, the captain started the engine and moved the boat away from the dock.

They quickly reached the Chesapeake Bay
and the captain let Doodle help raise the sail.

The gentle breeze rocked the boat back and forth,
and soon Doodle fell asleep.

When the boat ride was over, Doodle helped the Captain tie the boat back up to the dock.

The Captain shook Doodle's paw
and thanked him for his help.

As the sun set over the waters of the great
Chesapeake Bay, Doodle and his family headed home.

It had been a wonderful day -

and it was a day Doodle would always remember!

For Parents / Teachers / and All Caring Adults

Following are suggested discussion questions to nurture the joy of discovery in the children in your life. Their answers are guaranteed to surprise and delight!

How can you tell that Doodle is a special member of the family?

How do dogs show us unconditional love?

How many different types of boats can you name?

What did Doodle and the children do when they met the midshipman at the Naval Academy gate?

How do the students play croquet?

Why is the State House special?

What kind of books would you like to find in a bookstore?

What kind of treat do you think the shop owner gave Doodle?

Why did Doodle and his family cross the street where all the lines were?

Why did Doodle and his family wear life jackets on the sailboat?

How does someone get to be a captain on a boat?

What did Doodle do to help the captain?

What new things did Doodle and his family discover in Annapolis?

What new things will you discover tomorrow?

Annapolis

established 1649